Snake
AND THE
Doctor

DERRICK REYNOLDS

authorHOUSE·

AuthorHouse™
1663 Liberty Drive
Bloomington, IN 47403
www.authorhouse.com
Phone: 833-262-8899

Published by AuthorHouse 05/23/2022

ISBN: 978-1-6655-6005-4 (sc)
ISBN: 978-1-6655-6004-7 (e)

Library of Congress Control Number: 2022909178

Print information available on the last page.

Any people depicted in stock imagery provided by Getty Images are models,
and such images are being used for illustrative purposes only.
Certain stock imagery © Getty Images.

This book is printed on acid-free paper.

CONTENTS

CHAPTER 1

In August, this Lady named Jessie who likes to go camping. She headed to Oklahoma for a camping trip. The lake she decided on was Lake Fort Gibson. When she got there, the weather started to change, clouds came up, the weather turned bad, big rain drops, then hail started dropping, Jessie was in a heavy duty tent then the weather calmed down. So Jessie went to sleep and curled up like a baby and slept well. In the middle of the night a snake made its way into her tent, and she didn't know it. I need you to use your imagination Jessie had on a pretty gown that was wide open In the front, basically in the nude the snake entered her body the snake was small at the time.

The next morning Jessie woke up feeling good so she went on a walk when she got a mile away her stomach started to hurt so bad she had to sit down. Jessie's pain was on her left side. Jessie being from Michigan was used to cold weather and pain.

The area she camped at was Hammer Point, on Lake Banana Point in Oklahoma. So she headed back to the camp as she got closer to camp she was feeling better. Jessie sat in her reclining seat resting and trying to figure out why her stomach was hurting so much. That evening Jessie had a taste for some catfish so she drove to Wagoner, OK to get some catfish. It was about 1:00 PM when she got back to her camping site. Mary still didn't know she was penetrated by a snake, we will call him snake JR in the story. Jessie arrived on Friday, it's now Sunday morning Jessie laying on her back in her tent. Jessie doesn't have any kids, not married. She starts to feel cramps she knew she went through menopause, so she went back into town in Wagoner, to Wal-Mart looking for some medicine to help her with cramps.

After arriving back to her tent, unloading some groceries she picked up. Jessie took a shower after returning from the store. The snake that entered her body was starting to get hungry, he was swimming from her left side to her right side. Jessie was in excruciating pain, she started to Holla, no one heard her, so she took some medicine It stopped the pain. It was dinner time so Jessie cooked herself some eggs, then drank a large glass of milk. Guess what this was the snake's favorite meal, he hadn't had anything like this before, so he's happy now he made it back to his sleeping spot in Jessie's stomach.

CHAPTER 2

Jessie thought I should head back to Michigan but I have paid for this trip for a week. I'm not going nowhere; I will tough it out. The morning finally arrived it's Tuesday. Jessie calls Michigan to talk to friends and family. She talks to her friend Pam about her trip to Oklahoma, which hadn't gone well so far. Jessie said I have been bothered by severe pain, her friend Pam said you aren't pregnant are you. Jessie said, no I'm past menopause, something feels like it's in my stomach, maybe I'm just imagining it. Her friend tells her to pack up and head back to Michigan, she tells her friend I will think about it.

Jessie called another one of her friends Chris, they were friends since 1st grade. Her friend says hi Jessie how is the camping trip going, she said Chris I have been sick the entire time I have been having severe cramps. I bought medicine and I'm not pregnant I'm pass menopause. Jessie told Chris that she had walked the trails, and was riding her bicycle when she felt the pain the first time. Her friend Chris told her if she continues to feel bad to come home. Jessie said to herself "I need to make a couple more calls." She called her brother Jeff. He said Hello sister, how's the trip going? She lied to him because he would come down and make her come back home. Jessie said. "I'm having so much fun in Oklahoma at Lake Banana Point."

He said, "I'm glad you're doing okay, he said I know you have your gun,"

She said, "Yes, I got it, today is Thursday." She told her brother "I'm coming home Sunday evening."

He said, "Okay I love you." then hung up.

Jessie said, "I need to call my friend Tiffany. I know she is thinking of me, but hadn't called because she is giving me privacy. My friend Tiffany and her mom Lavern called to check on me."

They said, "be careful" before they got off the phone. Lavern said, "God Loves You!!!"

Jessie decided not to tell Tiffany how bad she had been feeling. Then Tiffany and Lavern said call us, we're here for you. Jessie said I'm feeling bad on this trip. Today is Friday and the sun is shining. This is the best I have felt all week. I think I'm

4

going fishing today. Let me get my fishing poles out of my truck. I wonder what fish is biting today. I think I will crappie fish today. This species of fish is hard to catch and picky about what color jig they will bite (jig) is a fake bait that looks like a baby fish. They sell them in yellow, red, white, purple, black, and orange. They come in many different colors. Jessie said I'm starting with a black and orange jig today.

CHAPTER 3

So Jessie walked to the water. At Hammer point It has a lot of rocks, so Jessie fell on a loose rock cut her elbow, she just dusted the dirt off of herself. She didn't get hurt, she looked and saw that she had broken her orange & black jig. So when she arrived at the water, she replaced the same Jig that broke orange and black.

In Jessie's first cast she hooked a monster crappie, she fought and fought and finally got the fish in, it was a trophy catch, people standing around looking and taking pictures. The news team just happened to be there. They put Jessie on the Sports News Channel that night and boy was she happy, Jessie called back to Michigan to tell her brother's friend Robert, who was a fisherman, he told her he wanted to go back with her next year when she goes back to Oklahoma.

Jessie caught a couple more good size crappie. All those people standing around, mostly men, were asking her what color jig was she using, Jessie didn't wanna tell them. Sometimes it's your own secret, most people have to keep fishing to figure out what color the fish are biting. She finally told them it was an orange and black combination.

CHAPTER 4

Heading back to camp with her fish Jessie was thinking to herself, about cleaning her fish and eating them tomorrow despite being sick. With severe cramps Just as Jessie started cooking the fish she caught, the snake in her stomach is getting hungry, he wants eggs, and a glass of milk, that was his first breakfast, lunch and dinner that's what he expects to eat. Jessie cooking fish isn't going to go well with the snake, so Jessie sat down to eat her fish and French fries and salad for 35 minutes.

The pain hit her really hard Jessie was screaming loudly when the park ranger heard her. He ran to see what was happening he said are you alright she said no. What's wrong ma'am, she said I am having a sharp pain on my left side, and pain on the right side of my stomach. The snake was mad because Jessie didn't cook eggs and gave him a glass of milk. So the snake started to swim in her stomach like a fish, going side to side and up and down, throwing his tail with an attitude so the ranger called the ambulance. Jessie took Jessie to the hospital. Jessie's trip to Oklahoma has really turned out bad, but she would not call her friends, she didn't want to worry them. Once she got to the Hospital, they did some x-rays, they came back negative. The doctor said I think you have bacteria in your stomach. They started to treat her for a bacterial infection. The snake started to feel something hot, the snake ran to the corner of Jessie's stomach and rolled into a ball to avoid the antibiotic. The snake was mad but felt hopeless in a ball, the snake thinking it's going to be over for me soon I'm going to die. They kept Jessie overnight but she started feeling better so they released her. Jessie returned to her campsite and called her brother saying that she had to go to the hospital. He told her to stay there, he's on his way, he arrived at record time. Jessie told her brother can we just stay one more night. Her brother said it couldn't hurt anything. They talked about old times when they were kids, laughing and having a good time so they fell asleep. The next morning it was time to head back to Michigan. They started eating breakfast, she cooked eggs and bacon and also had a glass of milk. The snake came out of the corner really happy because the **snake loves eggs, and milk. Even Jessie had a pep in her step and everyone's happy today. The brother packed all her belongings up and put them in her truck. Then they took off Jessie said what a trip to Oklahoma.**

CHAPTER 5

Once they arrived in Michigan it's Monday morning, Jessie had 3 more vacation days left. She just wanted to rest. The medicine Jessie was taking is all gone. Jessie likes watching a football game all of sudden, Jessie said it felt like she had to use the bathroom, but nothing was coming out. But she still felt like she had to pee, actually the snake was wanting out but was trapped in her dark stomach. The snake really had a hard time when Jessie drank Coca Coca. It makes the snake feel bad. In order for the snake to feel better it had to go in the corner of Jessie's stomach and roll up in a tight ball.

It's now December and it's very cold, snowy and ice. Jessie loves cold weather. Jessie is an all-around lady, she likes the cold weather. Wednesday noon Jessie was sitting on her patio singing. The snake was really getting nervous from the noise, so the snake gave out a snake hissing noise. Jessie heard it but thought she was hearing things. So she started singing again until she got tired then stopped. The snake made a loud hissing sound again, then Jesse put her head as close to her stomach as she could and said Is anyone in there? let me know so the snake hissed again. Jessie got excited because her friend was in her stomach. Jessie was going to keep this big secret to herself about the snake, every night she would talk to the snake all the snake did was hiss, but Jessie started to understand snake talk, she figured out that the snake likes eggs and a glass of milk just from the snake talk. She would talk to the snake like she was talking to a human, Jessie told the snake she is gaining weight and didn't know why the snake responded with his long hisses to Jessie. The snake said I'm gaining weight also. He said to Jessie, I give you permission to cook me a baked potato tonight and Jessie said I would do that for you.

CHAPTER 6

The snake controls Jessie because she doesn't have any kids and gets lonely a lot. Jesse thinks the snake is her first kid. Jessie's stomach problems stopped because the snake was happy. One evening Jessie got a phone call from the doctor in Oklahoma. The doctor asked her how she was feeling and she said she was fine. The doctor said I was looking through some old x-rays and came across yours. I need you to come back to Oklahoma so we can talk. Jessie said we are on the phone, let's talk. The doctor said it's a little more serious than that. Jessie said let me have your phone number then I'm going to call you back, after getting off the phone with the Doctor from Oklahoma, she started talking to the snake she said they want me to go back to Oklahoma. The Doctor found something in my stomach, the snake started to hiss, and hiss and hiss. Jessie said I know how to read the snake. The snake said to her, don't go back to Oklahoma, they just want to put you on more medication.

Jessie said to the snake you're right I'm not going back to Oklahoma they are using me for my money, plus I don't want them to know about our relationship (snake) and the snake said yes you're right. Today is Saturday. It's been snowing all day. It's time for the winter ball. That's where everyone in town comes to the Ball, Guess what Jessie had a hot date for the Ball, Jessie sat In her chair leaned forward and said hello to the snake are you there, and the snake hissed to Jessie I'm hear. She said to the snake I know you are going to get mad but I must tell you I have a date for the dance tonight the snake hissed I thought you cared about me, the snake said call the date off Jessie, she said okay I will do that, her dates name is Carl, he was excited about asking Jessie to the dance so when she called him and said I can't make it to the dance tonight I don't feel well, Carl said I bought a brand new suit It was for you Jessie. Then Jessie said, bye Carl then hung up the phone the snake hissed and said that was beautiful you really care about me.

CHAPTER 7

The weekend was over, It's Monday morning Jessie got another call. It was the Doctor from Oklahoma. Jessie's first word was I told you I'm not interested In coming back to Oklahoma, the Doctor said that's okay I drove to Michigan Jessie said, you gotta be kidding me. The Doctor said I need to talk with you again about your X-rays. In the Doctor's office I have your old X-rays from August, and now It's December. Would you meet in Dr. MOUNTAIN'S office? In the morning at 9:00am, she agreed to meet him. The next day Tuesday comes Jessie meets the Doctor from Oklahoma, In Dr. Mountain's medical office In Michigan, The Doctor from Oklahoma tells Jessie I have studied your X-ray about 50 times, there seems to be something in your stomach that looks like a worm. Jessie said I don't believe that you should stop harassing me. Then Jessie runs out of the Doctor's office really upset knowing that the Doctor was talking about her little friend inside her stomach. Thinking about what the Doctor said Jessie continues to get madder and madder.

Today Is Wednesday Jessie didn't hear from the Doctor so she was calm, so she went to work. Jessie went home ate dinner then fell asleep. Today a couple days later It's Friday Jessie's favorite day of the week. Jessie decided to eat Golden Corral, She got her plate and sat down and started to eat, and guess what happened next, out of nowhere here comes the Doctor from Oklahoma again. He just happened to be eating at the same place. The Doctor just sat down with Jessie, he didn't ask if it was okay to sit there he just started talking. Jessie said Excuse me, I need to make a phone call. The Doctor said okay, so she got up, walked to the other room and called the police. Jessie said it's a guy in the restaurant harassing me." Jessie was gone for about five minutes, she stood by the door until the police arrived. Yes, they were two big police officers. They entered Golden Corral Jessie told the police It's a Doctor from Oklahoma he keeps stalking me. I have told him a couple times to stay away from me. Jessie told the police I got sick in Oklahoma he helped me there, But he followed me back to Michigan, the Police arrested the Doctor for harassment. The poor Doctor was just trying to help her, Jessie watched as they put the Doctor Inside the Police car, she felt bad for what she had done but was tired of being followed, that night after having the Doctor arrested she started cramping again, she leaned over to her stomach, and said are you there? Hello, Hello, Hello. And no one answered, the snake was sick and couldn't hiss feeling bad. Jessie thought her friend was gone and she cried for two hours straight until she heard the hissing noise that she was used to.

The snake hissed and hissed. Go cook me some eggs, and get me a glass of milk. I fill weak and hungry, the snake said something was moving around In my stomach. Jessie said, let me feed you then you can get some rest and the snake said okay.

CHAPTER 8

Jessie was thinking, 2 weeks later, thinking about how much bad luck she has had In the last 3 months, Jessie decided to go wash her truck to get her mind off those problems so Jessie pulls Into the Car Wash, and start to wash her truck she finished her truck, It was shining like new money, she pulls Into the corner of the car wash where she starts to dry her truck off then a car pulls up next to her,and someone gets out of the car wearing dark sunglasses they said hello Jessie, and she said Hello back to them, Jessie was wondering who could know her at the carwash the person removed there sunglasses. It was the Doctor from Oklahoma again, he was released from Jail that day. Jessie immediately hit her emergency button on her phone then here comes the Police rolling in and they arrested him again. This poor Doctor just won't learn.

The wife of the Doctor heard about his second arrest but wasn't able to go see him, so Jessie goes to Oklahoma to see his wife, when she goes to the doctor's house. Jessie told the wife about her husband's arrest and he was told to stay away from me but he didn't. Jessie was really moved by what the Doctor's wife said, he was trying to save your life. It was December 16, 11:30 AM Jessie received a letter to appear in court, when that day came to go to court, Jessie entered the courtroom. She had to explain all day what had happened to her. The court sentenced the Doctor to five years in prison. He has a wife and two children and the wife doesn't work.

His wife screamed, ``What are we supposed to do as they took the Doctor out of court handcuffed and headed to Prison "The Doctor "Screamed I was just trying to save her life! This was eating Jessie up not sleeping at night. It was a tough decision but Jessie went back to the Police station to find out what Prison they sent the Doctor to. Before finding the prison Jessie returned to Oklahoma again to visit the Doctor's wife, when she arrived, they talked and Jessie gave the wife 5,000 dollars because she knew the wife wasn't working, Jessie said she was going to visit the Doctor In Prison, then Jessie said that she was going to get a Lawyer for the Doctor because her conscience was eating her up they were sitting In some very comfortable chairs talking under the Doctor's shade tree, while sitting and talking they saw a snake in the grass. The Doctor's wife got scared. Jessie said leave it alone it will leave on its own. In the meantime Jessie's shirt was just jumping around, she told the Doctor's wife she has a nervous stomach. The snake saw one of his cousin's In the grass inside of Jessie's stomach but couldn't get to him. That's why he was going side to side in her stomach because he couldn't get out of her stomach. Remember when Jessie went to Oklahoma the first time that's how she got the snake in her stomach.

When Jessie got ready to leave, the Doctor's wife headed back to Michigan. When Jessie drove off she started hearing that hissing sound so she pulled off the road, leaned over to her stomach and the snake said, turn around go back. That snake was my cousin, so Jessie turned around to go back to see if they could find the snake.

CHAPTER 9

The snake In her stomach, when she got back to the house, they looked everywhere for the snake but couldn't find him. Jessie said I wonder where I would have put the snake if we would have found it. So Jessie headed back to Michigan she stopped at I hop for breakfast when she got back from Oklahoma, she ordered some eggs and a glass of milk to make the snake happy because that is his favorite meal, when Jessie left I-Hope she stopped at a couple of garage sales, the first garage sale she stopped at their were some fake snakes sitting on the counter she bought a couple of those plastic snakes, and a couple of shirts and a pair of pants, Jessie was happy with her purchases so she went home to get some rest, before she went to sleep Jessie put those plastic snakes on top of the TV, so when she has visitors they can see those 2 pretty blue and yellow snakes.

While Jessie was trying to sleep she was tossing and turning because the snake In her stomach was agitated because she bought those plastic snakes at the garage sale, the snake was jealous because he wants to be # 1. The snake continued to hiss and move around In her stomach for about an hour, until It settled down then Jessie went to sleep.

Today Is Friday Jessie's favorite day, so she decided to treat herself to something nice so she went to the music store. Once she got in there It was so much to pick from, Jessie tried Instruments after, Instruments she was in the Music Store for 2 hours then she decided on a set of drums, a harmonica, and a trumpet after finishing her purchases she spent $10,500 on her purchases. She had It delivered and set up for Friday, after they set everything up Jessie started playing the drums. The snake In her stomach went crazy. The snake was thinking Jessie was trying to kill it. The snake was swimming and diving and diving all over her stomach. The noise was excruciating to the snake, Jessie finally stopped playing the music for the night and started reading how to play Instruments, and read music because Jessie was planning to join a music group If she could get better on her Instruments.

The next day Jessie went to the Doctor because of bad stomach aches. The Doctor was wanting to give her some Antibiotics Jessie said I used them before but the pain came back again. The Doctor said let's do another round of Antibiotics to see if that helps.

Jessie decided after the Doctor's visit she wasn't going to take the Antibiotics, she started thinking about the Doctor that she sent to prison for trying to help her. Driving about 35mph all of sudden she had a flat she pulled over but didn't know how to change a flat. Jessie was about 30 minutes from home so she called her brother. He came to change her flat he said to Jessie, why do your stomach look twisted on your right side. Jessie told her brother she hurt herself at work but that wasn't really true, the snake is starting to get big for some reason.

The next morning Jessie headed to the Prison where the Doctor was to get her on the waiting list, she hadn't seen him In 3 years once Jessie got permission from the Prison to visit, she went back to visit the Doctor from Oklahoma, she had dreamed about him for 3 days In a row all she could think about was the Doctor wanted to bring her to the hospital to do a x-ray on her stomach he saw something very small In her stomach, he went to Prison for traveling to Michigan to help me, also he stalked me asking to meet him In the hospital after the third time he was arrested and sent to Prison. While In Prison he started aging. The second day In Prison a Prisoner beat the Doctor up. He didn't know how to fight because he was a Corporate Man not a fighter In Prison. The Doctor figured with everyone seeing him get beat up by a murderer. He started to work out in prison every day for a month, the Doctor got buffed, he had big muscles. Now the prisoners were scared of the Doctor. The Doctor was propositioned to be a head gang member because of his massive size. Even though he was getting so much attention, he continued to study his medical books, because he wants to go back to work one day because he's only 50 years old. Today is the big day Thursday 11:00am Jessie enters the prison she walks in. These big strong steel doors closed behind her, she made her way to the information desk, the things they put her through, stripped, searched her clothes off, they padded her down. The jailers are mean they treated her like she was a prisoner, Jessie started to cry because she realized she had a guy in jail that shouldn't be there. Finally after 1 hour Jessie finally arrived in the visitors room. It took 20 minutes before the prisoner's arrived in the visitor's room. Because they had to pad her down so she didn't bring any weapons in the visitor's room.

CHAPTER 10

The prisoner's came in one by one, the Doctor was the third Prisoner to enter the room. Jessie was still looking at the door because she remembered the doctor being a small man, the Doctor walked around looking for Jessie because she had gained over 50 pounds in those 4 years, The doctors had to ask the prison guard who was his visitor, the guard said the lady sitting in the corner he headed over to her, once he figured out who she was the lady who had him put in prison. He said "what are you doing here, she was scared to speak to him because the doctor was so big with those massive muscles.

Once she got herself together she said hi, I am so sorry for what happened to you that's why I'm here to right my wrong. I got a lawyer 2years ago trying to get you out. The doctor says this is 4 years later and I'm still here. Jessie says the Lawyer was very expensive but he's supposed to be really good. The Doctor from Oklahoma asked her do you know what I have been through since I have been in this dump. I was beaten up my second day in prison. I have been on lock down for 45 days, dark and lonely and my wife divorced me, Jessie started to cry and cry. Then she told the Doctor she would make it right.

Jessie returned home, sat on her couch then started to brainstorm about her future. One more thing she wanted to do on her bucket list was to return back to Oklahoma. To camp because 4 years ago it was a disaster. As she sat there at that point she decided to head back to Oklahoma Friday Morning which is one of her happiest days of her life.

Today is Thursday Jessie is packing her clothes, and gathering her fishing gear to fulfill her last bucket list.

It's Friday morning, Jessie takes off heading back to Oklahoma, she tells know one she gassed up but the weather was beginning to cool off. It's September 20, she arrives at Hammer Point Lake Banana about 9:30pm. Then Jessie get set up. It took her about an hour to get everything set up, then she went to sleep. It was Saturday morning she woke up feeling refreshed so she went for a walk just looking at the beautiful lake. People were very friendly speaking to each other. After a long walk, she returns to the camp then begins to cook dinner. She started with one of her favorites: a big pot of chili beans, and dinner is ready quickly. She was ready

26

to eat the chili beans, and crackers with a little hot sauce, she kept saying to herself, "This is so good.".

Things could not be going better for Jessie, nothing happening bad at all today. It's Wednesday she goes for a boat ride with a couple she met when she went for a walk.

Jessie was just laughing having a good time on the boat, they ate lunch on the boat. They even swam for a while on the other side of the lake. It's time to head back to camp, it's late evening when they arrived back at the campsite. The couple asked Jessie if she wanted to go fishing tomorrow morning with them at about 5:00 AM, Jessie said she would love too.

The alarm clock goes off at 4:30 AM, Thursday morning time to get ready for the fishing trip with her new friends. Being excited Jessie knew she was leaving Friday, after a week of fun.

The couple and Jessie took off in the boat seeking crappie and Bass, they pulled up to a cove. It was a little windy but it didn't stop the fish from biting. They caught eight bass, and 10 crappie. They were really big in the first 30 minutes. They stayed for 2 hours and caught 30 fish, 10 bass, and 20 crappie. Everyone was happy but tired. They headed back to camp because they had to clean the fish. They decided to have a fish fry and invited some of the other campers to join. They made it back, started cleaning fish, and cutting potatoes. They made a big bowl of salad. The fish was done a total of eight couples joined, they ate and ate until everyone got up and started dancing and singing, that's what Jessie likes, when the party was over. They planned to make this an annual event every October 20, annually we will all meet here next year. They agree everyone hugged and went their separate ways.

The next morning Jessie woke up, Friday it's time to go home, and it's her happiest day of the week, she started packing up her things. It wouldn't take her very long, approximately 30 min to get everything packed up, just before driving off. Jessie's shirt started blowing up and down and her stomach started hurting. What a bad blow after a whole week of no problems then this happened. Jessie turns her car off, then she hears the hissing sound again. Jessie dropped her head and listened to the snakes hissing.

CHAPTER 11

The snake said, "Jessie, don't ever come back here again. Then Jessie said we're going on this camping trip every year." Then the snake got really mad, and started rolling around In her stomach. So Jessie was hurting and drove off really fast, she drove all day then the snake finally calmed down. Jessie made it back to Michigan at 10:30 PM, she headed straight home.

Today is Monday Jessie heads to her attorney's office, trying to get the Doctor from Oklahoma out of prison, her attorney told her he had good news, the Doctor getting out because Covid-19 helped get the Doctor out of prison for 8,300 dollars Jessie wrote the Lawyer a check. She was just smiling and excited, so Jessie and her attorney headed to the prison. It was about 1 hour drive. They arrived and went through the process to get the Doctor out, he didn't know she was getting HIM out today the jailers went to his cell, they said to the DOCTOR you're getting out.

They gather his belongings so fast it's not like he had a lot of stuff. Once he was ready to walk out the prison all the prisoners were shouting his name yelling, it's your going away party. The Doctor walks up to the attorney, shakes his hand and says Thank

You, then looks over to Jessie, and says Thank you, and I forgive you. I remember you said you would make it right, thank you again.

While on their way back to Michigan after being released from Jail, the Doctor says where do I go? I'm divorced, my ex-wife got married while I was locked up. Jessie said, I will get you a hotel for a week. Then we will figure it out. They arrived at the Hotel which was close to Jessie's house, then the attorney took Jessie to her car which was parked at the Attorney's Office Jessie got in her car and went home.

At the end of the week it was the doctor's last day in the hotel, Jessie took her extra car to the doctor Jessie headed to her house. She told the Doctor she was going to the grocery store to get some food. Jessie asked the doctor what he wanted from the store and he said watermelon.

Jessie says okay and leaves for the grocery store. Jessie was shopping in the grocery store, it was full of customers. She was in the store for about an hour. Jessie's stomach started to hurt again really bad, then she passed out in the store. They called the ambulance, and they rushed her to the hospital. The doctors decided she needed an emergency surgery. They cut her stomach open. The Doctor was scared they would see this big snake in her stomach. They keep a fire gun in the Emergency Room, it gets really hot if you turn it up high fire comes out, they use it to burn nails off fingers or toes. The Doctor was holding the fire gun, ready to use it. The snake crawls out of Jessie's stomach, they were not sure if Jessie was going to live, when the snake came out they were going to shoot him with the fire gun but they didn't, because the snake fell to the ground then while lying on the floor, the snake started having some babies, the mother snake had a set of twins, a twin boy and a twin girl who died as well. The staff was stunned. They put the mom and the twins In a big box and took them to the refrigerator where they keep human bodies. The Doctor was able to save Jessie when she awoke, they told Jessie you had a big snake In your stomach who had babies Jessie started yelling those are my babies where are they? I want to see my babies. They told her they died. The Doctor's wanted to know how this happened Jessie was so out of control they wheeled her down to see the snakes. They were in a box In the refrigerator. Jessie said, "DO NOT MOVE THOSE SNAKES!"

Jessie calls the Doctor from Oklahoma, who was at her house to tell him he was wondering where she was. The last time they were together yesterday she told the Doctor she was going to the grocery store the Doctor hadn't seen her since. The Doctor from Oklahoma arrives at the hospital to check on Jessie, she starts to explain to the Doctor what happened. The Doctor from Oklahoma said to her this is what I was trying to tell you, I saw something on the x-ray machine, then he said I went to prison for being right the entire time!

Jessie told the Doctor from Oklahoma that she was going to have a funeral for her babies, he said are you kidding me! Then she said, "No, I'm not.". Jessie got out of the hospital then they released the snakes to her the next day Tuesday afternoon when they left the hospital. They went to the funeral home to plan for a funeral. The Funeral Home said, this would be our first ever Funeral for a snake, the funeral is set for Thursday morning at 11:00am, they will have caskets for all three snakes.

Today is Thursday morning, It's time for the Funeral. Jessie went all out for the snakes, she had a full escort from the Police Department. SIRENS BLARING, people standing on the side of the road like if the President of the United States had died, people everywhere standing on fences, sitting in chairs, on bridges, fast foods closed down for the funeral. The Lawyer who got the Doctor from Oklahoma out of prison attended the funeral. This was a different kind of funeral, they played music Jessie was crying. I lost my babies, people were consoling Jessie at the Funeral, they buried the snakes at the pet cemetery.

CHAPTER 12

It took Jessie about two weeks to get herself together after the funeral. The next week Jessie and the Doctor from Oklahoma got married. The Doctor from Oklahoma promised Jessie to get her a pet snake so they can raise it together, Jessie agreed but wanted a White Snake.

The new couple was happy, guess what, Jessie got pregnant with a real baby, Jessie had a boy, 8 pound 6 ounces. Jessie named the baby boy SNAKE ROBINSON, the couple talked about raising the newborn along with the white snake. The snake had a box, this was new to his human brother. They named the Snake. White Johnson. They loved each other, the baby could look through the box to see his snake brother. The new family is so obsessed with the Snake. They made an agreement that the snake would come to the babysitter also, Jessie agreed to pay for both kids, and the young babysitter agreed.

When the boys got three months old, the human boy went for his check up, everything checked out okay. So Jessie and her husband from Oklahoma took the snake for his check up, and the veterinarian said we must take his teeth out and defang him so he won't bite anyone. The snake had surgery that lasted one hour.

When it was completed, the snake was really happy. The following Sunday the entire family went to church, the family carrying their box with the Snake inside of it but no one knew what was in it. Everything was fine until the music started playing, the snake would move around hissing. The snake slipped out of the box.

Just before getting home, from Church the snake was just about a mile from home, he had to cross a field. It was a tall tree in the middle of the field, beside the tree was a very long tall black snake, with yellow eyes. It was almost as long as the tree. It started chasing the snake. He was hissing, hissing, hissing and hissing, the only way he got away was when he went under the fence, and the big snake was way too big to get under the fence. The little snake on the other side of the fence with his tail gave the big snake a finger and said you big freaking bully.

The snake knocked on the door, when he arrived home crying and bleeding, saying, Mom, Mom! Jessie opened the door screaming and crying, My baby is back! The Doctor from Oklahoma runs to the door, and says he's back.

They bring the snake in clean him up, later that afternoon, they put bars on his cage, and put a tracking device on the snake.

This is the state fair time, it's the first time for the human baby and the baby snake. The Fair starts Friday and today is Wednesday. Everyone is excited about the fair. It's the big day, It's Fair time. Today, Friday, the snake gets sick, breaks out with bumps all over his face, and his head swells to the size of a golf ball. They rushed him to the Veterinarian.

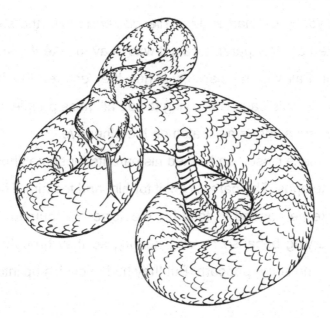

They tell Jessie and her husband, the snake has diabetes, and he's going to go blind, we're going to try to save his life. The Vet says he has to have surgery right now. They agreed. The snake goes into surgery for two hours, before the surgery is over the Doctor comes out and says I have some bad news to the family. We had to take his right eye and possibly the left eye, and he could go blind in time. Both parents were crying, they said we understand Doctor. Do what you have to do to save his life. The snake comes out of surgery, they have to wait for three more days before they can pick him up.

The parents went home to discuss the snake's home health care. So they hired a 13-year-old girl for $20.00 per hour. They hired her for everyday after school to talk to the snake and sing to him to keep the snake calm.

The young girl named Michelle wanted to take the snake to the State Fair. Her parents said it was okay to take the snake to the State Fair with his parents. When they entered the fair, the snake in his little cage was trying to see all those people, blind in one eye and a very small patch on the other eye.

The snake hissed and asked his parents for some chocolate, and some eggs. The parents got it for him and fed him. They told the snake he needed to take his medicine. His human brother started crying because he was hungry, so they brought him a corndog and some popcorn. But they had to cut his up into small pieces.

It was time to go home, because the snake was lying on his right side, it meant he was tired, and ready to go home. The girl rode two rides by herself when they got into the car, the snake's parents gave her 75.00 dollars then she said thank you. They dropped her off at home and she said, I see you Monday after school. The snake was mad because the girl had to go home.

CHAPTER 13

The boys are both 16 years old. The human boy, and the snake. The human boy's girlfriend has one arm. The family really loves his girlfriend and they take her on vacations with the family. They were willing to buy her a prosthetic, but the girlfriend didn't want one.

The son got his girlfriend pregnant, they had a baby girl, she was gorgeous with red hair. Both sets of grandparents on both sides were so happy.

The snake was very jealous because he wants a girlfriend too, so he started figuring out how to run away again, but this time going out to look for a girlfriend. The Human brother's baby hates the snake and she is 2 years old now, she throws water on the snake and hits the cage all the time. It was 12:00pm in the morning, Tuesday the snake had enough he lost weight so he could fit between the bars in his cage so he could escape. He is out of the cage, moves to the door squarm up the door, opens the door and leaves the house.

The snake is older and wiser. The first place he goes to was I-hop, hanging out in the back by the trash can so he can get some of the leftovers. The first night the snake gets a big dinner of his eggs he also found some orange juice. He was really happy so he slept under the dumpster.

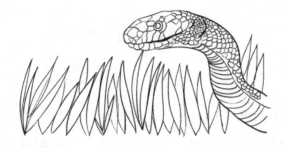

The next morning the snake eased his way down the alley looking at the tall buildings. The noises had him scared but he maintained his composure, so he won't panic and get caught again. The snake ended up at the Zoo which was 5 miles from where he lives. Getting farther and farther away from his home. When the snake entered the Zoo, the snake wound up in the elephant's cage. He had to be extremely careful, so that the 2000 pound elephant didn't smash him; the snake slept under the hay In the corner.

In the morning when the Zoo workers fed the elephants, the snake would eat the leftovers from the elephants. The snake took an afternoon stroll in the field to get some sun, while lying next to the tree, something went by the tree very slowly, but came back again even closer to the tree. It was a pretty yellow and red snake, really skinny but long. The boy snake hissed and said Hello Cutie, and the female snake said, Hello, would you like to go for a stroll down the sidewalk in the woods where the snake couples hang out? He said, I would love to come.

CHAPTER 14

The snakes hit it off and she asked the snake if he would stay the night with her, he didn't know anything about a girl. He agreed, and they kissed that night. Then they became boyfriend and girlfriend. The next morning he was so in love he didn't even eat breakfast, but when lunch came they ate McDonald's leftovers, after lunch they headed to the hills to overlook the city.

The snake started thinking about his family. He was getting home sick, so he explained to his girlfriend his situation, he told her he was headed home but would be back in a week. His girlfriend said no, if you leave I'm leaving with you. He agreed they would leave in the morning.

It's the morning, the snake couple heads back home, and a dog starts to chase them. They ran under a big rock until the German Shepherd left. They had to stay there all night, it was late and they were hungry.

They found a chocolate cupcake, and they began to eat it. His girlfriend starts to get choked. The snake does mouth to mouth, he sticks his tongue down her throat to dislodge the chocolate. His girlfriend got mad for the first time. She says I have never got choked in my entire life. The next morning they continued their journey back to the snake's house. They were about 5 miles from his house, then some kid outside saw the snakes and they started chasing them so they crawled under this vacant house. They were safe for about 15 minutes, until another snake came under the house, and started flirting with the snake's girlfriend. The snake under the house challenged the snake to a fight to see who took the pretty girlfriend. Remember the snake was blind in one eye.

The snake told his girlfriend I'm not losing you to another snake so they started fighting. The snake's girlfriend saw him getting his butt kicked early under the house. Things started to turn in the blind snake's favor, the other snake started getting tired and slowing down. The poor boyfriend with one eye started ripping him apart, dragging him in the mud, hitting him in the head, until the snake was unconscious. Then the boyfriend told his girlfriend let's go. They were fighting in the dark. It was really, really dark where they came from under the pretty vacant white house. They continued on their way home again. They traveled until the morning, they were about a mile from home all they had to do was to cross the train tracks.

CHAPTER 15

They attempted to cross the tracks, the trains horn was sounding really loud. Just when the girlfriend was almost halfway across the track, she stopped, frightened from the loud horn of the train. Her boyfriend came back quickly to help his girlfriend off the tracks. The train is coming fast he grabs her but the train is already there the train cuts off some of her tail, leaving her screaming, hissing and crying at the same time. The boyfriend says `` I need to get you to my mom's house fast.

They reach the house, the snake hits the door loudly. The snake mother Jessie comes to the door but she wasn't excited to see him like the last time he ran away. He says Mom, I have a surprise for you. He kept his girlfriend at the side of the porch. His mom said I have been really mad at you, we decided we aren't going to let you come back home. He starts to cry. Thinking I have some explaining to do. I was jealous of my human brother, he had a girlfriend, and I didn't. And he also had a baby who didn't like me. I had a crush on the babysitter but she paid me no attention plus she couldn't like me anyway I am a snake. So I broke out to get a girlfriend. I love you mom, and dad. The snake said I had a surprise. He says to his girlfriend Come on out from behind the porch, here comes this pretty red and yellow snake, bleeding from the tail. The mom Jessie said Oh! My baby, what happened let's get you in the house to help you stop the bleeding,

That's how the snake got back in. He knew this was his last chance. The mom and dad from Oklahoma cleaned the girlfriend up when they finished and put them both in the cage.

The snake couple was in love, they convinced his parents they wanted to get married and the parents agreed. They planned the wedding. They had a special lady make a small dress for the girlfriend snake, and a tuxedo for the boy snake.

The lady measured both of the snakes, she was making the white dress and the white tuxedo, they were getting married Saturday. In their backyard with about 500 human guests, they brought some snakes from the pet store to attend, there were about 75 snakes in attendance. It was a beautiful wedding, they rented a bus for 75 snakes only. They took them all over town, they were watching a movie on the bus while the driver went on the highways for 2hours. The movie was showing snakes that was In LOVE. The snakes were just hissing with laughter. It was time to go, and most of the snakes started crying. Some of the snakes wanted to get married, others were crying because they didn't want to go back to the pet store.

CHAPTER 16

The couple is married and very happy. The parents were treating them nicely, 3 months later, the snake's wife got pregnant. The parents were happy, they didn't have any boys In the family in awhile. The human brother, and the snake brother are both 17yrs old now.

The human brother is talking about college next year, and the snake was glad because he and his beautiful snake wife will get all the attention. It was Valentine's day, the wife snake started throwing up, and laying around the parents took her to the Veterinarian. The office was full of animals and they had to wait for about two hours. Once they were called to the back, the pretty snake wife had thrown up three times in the lobby already.

The tech in the back said we need to do an x-ray because she is lethargic, and very pale. They take the snake to the x-ray room. Once they finished they asked the parents to come into this big empty room. They told the parents the snake is pregnant with twins. The parents were shocked. They said to the tech we understand so they paid the bill and headed home. They had a conversation with both snakes in the cage. We will support you, we're going to get you a bigger cage, and for the babies coming, we'll buy them some bunk beds.

The snakes started hissing and smiling. They told the wife snake we're going to take you to the Veterinarian to get your poison glands out, so you can't bite anyone so we don't get sued.

CHAPTER 17

Today is Friday, they take the snake's wife to get defanged so she can't bite anyone. They finished while heading home, she wanted some ice cream so they stopped to get her a double scoop of Vanilla. She thanks them. When she got home, she went to bed. Her snake husband was watching her sleep, he was so in love with her. It was getting close for her to have the babies in one week. The babies were making her uncomfortable with pain hitting her, like human pain like having babies. It's time they take her to the Vet hospital to have the babies, her husband snake is rolling around, nervous and hissing very loud. They take her back to have the babies but no one could go back because of Covid-19. They didn't want the babies to catch Covid-19, the wife of the snake babies was born, she had a boy and a girl. They are really beautiful.

When the daddy snake saw his babies, he passed out in the pen, then came too in about 1 minute. He was so excited to see the babies. The parents take their family home, including the twin babies. They got home and turned the heat up in the house to keep the babies warm.

The babies cried all night, wanting milk from the mother, the human parents checked on them all through the night. The old babysitter, the young girl came to see the snake she babysitted for and his new wife and their little babies.

The young babysitter said she is going to shop for the new babies tomorrow. It started getting late and everyone went to sleep. The babysitter is bringing some gifts after she gets out of school.

The parents got some gifts for the babies. Everyone was enjoying the new babies, they are moving around well.

The snake dad wants to go out and get some gifts for his babies, so his parents let the dad out because he Is so excited to go get gifts for his babies. The dad snake has a little skateboard, he rides on it in the woods, and he goes to the store to get some presents. When heading home, the husband snake was crossing the railroad tracks, get's hit by a car and dies with the babies presents.

The word got back to snake parents, Jessie and the Doctor from Oklahoma, and everyone was distraught. The wife passed out, but came back too. She was so down from losing her snake husband and tired from the twin babies being born. They went to the funeral homes to make arrangements. The funeral is Saturday morning, at 10AM. Today is Tuesday, the family is really hurt.

CHAPTER 18

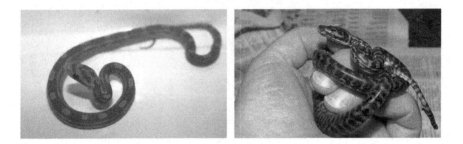

Today

Today is Saturday time for the funeral. The entire family was dressed in blue, including the wife and the babies were also in blue. This was a good dad who loved his family, friends and loved ones. They had a limousine for the Daddy snake, and his funeral home was standing room only. They buried the Daddy snake in the Pet Cemetery. The twin snakes got older and they tried to kill themselves a couple times because they felt they couldn't make it with their Daddy.

Stay Tuned

Part 2 is coming soon . . .

Printed in the United States
by Baker & Taylor Publisher Services